W9-BTF-180

Make way for more monsters from
MONSTER MANOR

MONSTER MANOR

Beatrice's Spells

by **PAUL MARTIN** and **MANU BOISTEAU**
Adapted by **LISA PAPADEMETRIOU**
Illustrated by **MANU BOISTEAU**

Hyperion Books for Children
New York

visit us at www.abdopublishing.com

Reinforced library bound edition published in 2012 by Spotlight,
a division of ABDO Publishing Group, 8000 West 78th Street, Edina,
Minnesota 55439. Spotlight produces high-quality reinforced library
bound editions for schools and libraries. This edition reprinted
by arrangement with Disney Book Group, LLC.

Printed in the United States of America, Melrose Park, Illinois.
052011
092011

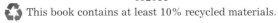
First published under the title *Maudit Manoir,*
Les Maléfices de Béatrice in France by Bayard Jeunesse.
© Bayard Editions Jeunesse, 2001 Text copyright © 2001 by Paul Martin
Illustrations copyright © 2001 by Manu Boisteau Monster Manor and the
Volo colophon are trademarks of Disney Enterprises, Inc.
Volo® is a registered trademark of Disney Enterprises, Inc.

Library of Congress Cataloging-in-Publication Data

This title was previously cataloged with the following information:

Martin, Paul, 1968-
Beatrice's spells / by Paul Martin and Manu Boisteau ;
adapted by Lisa Papademetriou ; illustrated by Manu Boisteau.
p.cm. -- (Monster Manor ; #3)
[1. Monsters --Juvenile fiction.]
I. Boisteau, Manu. II. Papademetriou, Lisa. III. Title. IV. Series.
PZ7.M3641833 Be 2003
[FIC]--dc22
                              2005295537

ISBN 978-1-59961-884-5 (reinforced library bound edition)

All Spotlight books are reinforced library bindings
and manufactured in the United States of America.

Contents

If you're ever in Transylvaniaville, be sure to stop by Mon Staire Manor. Everyone calls it *Monster* Manor... that's because a bunch of monsters live there.

The Haunted Hills

Nerdburg

Transylvaniaville

Malibu Nightclub

MALIBU

A Scary-looking Tree

The Slippen Falls

vi

There are lots of fun things to do at the Manor. You can stroll through the cemetery, watch the swamp glow under the moonlight, or make a few new friends!

The FEMUR Family

EYE-GORE & STEVE

This sweet little family may look scary, but the truth is that they have no guts at all.

They want to be skate punks, but they're really just zombies with bad attitudes.

BEATRICE Mon Staire

She's haunted by a horrible secret... and a hairdo that's even worse.

Wolf Man STU

When the moon is full, he becomes human. Well, *somewhat* human...

COUNT SNOBULA

He isn't rich, but he *is* totally stuck up. Thank goodness he sleeps all day.

Step through the gate—
let's see who's home!

The SWAMP HORROR

It ain't easy being a big green ball of toxic slime!

SALLY the Specter

Beatrice's mother is smart, sassy—and a ghost!

Professor VON SKALPEL

The most brilliant mad scientist in town. He's a real cutup.

FRANKIE

Created by Von Skalpel,
Frankie is one of a kind.
Thank goodness.

Beatrice will try to turn you into a toad!

CHAPTER ONE
What a Mess!

Mon Staire Manor was quiet and snuggly under a light blanket of snow. The only sign of life was a thin trail of smoke that crept up from the chimney. It was at moments like these that the villagers who lived nearby found it easy to believe that the Manor wasn't really haunted. They could almost trust that the folks who lived in Mon Staire Manor were normal people like you and me, and not vampires, werewolves, or giant balls of toxic slime.

That was just wishful thinking, of course.

No—Mon Staire Manor really *was* filled with strange creatures. The local people called it Monster Manor and stayed as far away from the house as possible.

The Manor was owned by Beatrice Mon Staire. Beatrice didn't love living with a bunch of monsters. Actually, she would have preferred to live alone. But the monsters paid her to live there (most of the time), and—hey—she needed the spending money. Lately, though, a few of them had been late with their rent checks. Not only that, but a full moon was coming soon. And all of the monsters had been acting crazy—making strange noises at all hours of the day and night. Beatrice was getting pretty sick of their commotion. That was why, when the sound of Count Snobula snoring in his crypt started getting on her nerves, Beatrice decided that it was the perfect day to do some tidying up in the attic.

"Ah, I'll finally get some peace and quiet," Beatrice said, as she trudged up the stairs. But the attic was an even bigger mess than she had remembered. "This is going to take all day!" she griped.

"Psst!" said a voice behind Beatrice.

Beatrice turned and saw her mother, Sally Specter, resting half on, half in the floor. Sally was a ghost, but she didn't like to think of herself as one. Admitting that she was dead would make her sound boring, she said.

Psst! behind you!

What's shakin'?

Mind if I hang out?

"Hey, toots!" Sally said.

"Mother!" Beatrice yelled. "How many times do I have to tell you not to hang through the floor? It's very alarming for the people in the room below to see your legs dangling out of the ceiling!"

"They should consider themselves lucky to see a pair of legs as good as mine!" Sally snapped. She floated up through the floor and dusted herself off, even so. "Hey!" she said, looking around the attic. "You aren't going to throw away any of my stuff, are you?"

"Uh . . . no," Beatrice lied.

"You're as bad at lying as you are at performing spells, sweetie," Sally told her daughter. "You really shouldn't do either without my supervision."

Beatrice rolled her eyes. Her mother could be such a nag. "Okay, okay," she admitted. "I'm going to clean up the attic and get rid of a few things." Beatrice looked around the attic and sighed. It was full of cobwebs. "I just wish that there were some way to toss out this junk without tearing through these gorgeous webs."

"Junk!" Sally exclaimed. "Why some of this junk must be worth a fortune!"

Beatrice grunted. "A fortune *cookie*, maybe," she grumbled. Beatrice inspected the piles of stuff that her tenants—not to mention several generations of her ancestors—had loaded into the cramped attic. There were thick, dusty books of magic spells, old Egyptian coffins, chipped crystal balls, bags and bags of eye of newt and toe of frog (all past their expiration dates), plus plenty of stuff that was an utter mystery. "Can't these monsters ever clean up after themselves?" Beatrice asked. "I always have to do all of the work around here!"

Beatrice began to make a pile of everything

that she was going to throw out. She tossed a few of Count Snobula's moldy old coffins onto the pile, next to Eye-Gore the zombie's collection of Night Worms albums. Then she threw a few things that had belonged to her parents onto the pile: a magic carpet that couldn't fly, a tub of stinkweed soap, a dented trumpet, a crusty tube of ancient toothpaste, and a pile of dirty underwear.

"I can't believe you're throwing away all of this great stuff!" Sally complained. "That underwear is still good!"

"Then *you* wash it," Beatrice suggested.

Sally didn't say anything.

"That's what I thought," Beatrice said. "I don't even want to touch it. I think I'll just do an empty-attic spell to get rid of all of this stuff."

Sally folded her arms across her chest. "This ought to be good," she mumbled. Sally knew that her daughter wasn't very good at spells.

Beatrice frowned and began to recite the spell. "*Alacazoom, alacazunk!* Salvation Army, come and pick up this junk!" she finished.

Nothing happened.

Sally giggled. "You should have paid attention when I tried to teach you my charms," she said.

"You have no charm," Beatrice snapped. She was annoyed that her spell hadn't worked. Then again, her spells almost never did. Beatrice was plain lousy at magic. "Besides, I . . . I wasn't really trying. I don't want to waste my powers on a silly little project like this. I'm sure that Frankie will be happy to take this stuff down to the thrift store for me." Frankie was Professor Von Skalpel's faithful assistant.

"Sure thing," Sally said. "But you may want to reconsider giving away some of these books of spells," she added, peering at the pile. "I think you could use them."

Beatrice grabbed a box full of junk and left the attic in a huff.

CHAPTER TWO
Monster Madness!

When Beatrice arrived at the bottom of the stairs, she came face to face with a huge, horrible, hideous monster. It was as wide as it was tall and oozed putrid-smelling green slime with every wet, squishing step it took.

"Horror!" Beatrice said to the monster. Horror was the monster's name—Swamp Horror. He lived in the radioactive swamp near the Manor.

"Hi, Beatrice," Horror said. "What have

you got there?" Horror reached for the dented trumpet that was sticking out of the cardboard box Beatrice was carrying.

"Oh, it's just garbage," Beatrice told him.

Horror wrapped his slimy lips around the trumpet and blew. A wet-sounding, sputtery *Sploot!* blasted through the Manor. "Do you mind if I keep this?" Horror asked.

"Sure, go ahead," Beatrice said as she headed down the hall. "I don't think anyone else is going to want it now," she added under her breath.

Horror blew on the trumpet again, unleash

ing a sound much like that of an elephant trapped in a barrel of snot.

Beatrice turned a corner and ran into a hairy werewolf. He let out a dangerous growl, showing his long fangs.

"What is it, Stu?" Beatrice demanded. "I have to find Frankie."

"Where is that horrible noise coming from?" Wolf Man Stu shouted. "Don't you people understand that I am a dangerous creature of the night? I need my beauty sleep."

"It's just Horror, practicing the trumpet," Beatrice said.

"The trumpet!" Stu cried. "I thought someone was trying to drown a goose in a vat of Jell-O! If that swamp thing thinks he can get away with this, he's got another think coming. . . ." Wolf Man Stu leaped away down the hall.

Beatrice watched him go, gritting her teeth. Whenever Stu and Horror got into a fight, there was always a huge mess of slime and fur to clean up. And *she* always got stuck with it. If I lived alone, Beatrice thought, I wouldn't have to clean up anyone's slime but my own!

Beatrice balanced the box on her hip and knocked on the door to the laboratory. A moment later, it swung open to reveal an enormous creature that had clearly been put together with mismatched body parts from the cemetery near the radioactive swamp. Beatrice gasped. But not because of the creature—that was just Frankie, Professor Von Skalpel's assistant. She gasped because Frankie was being held upside down by an enormous purple tentacle!

"Hi," Frankie said cheerfully.

"What is going on in here?" Beatrice

demanded. She peered behind Frankie to where Professor Von Skalpel stood. The professor was stirring a large cooking pot. Something huge and slimy tried to make an escape, and the professor poked at it with a fork. The slimy thing slipped back into the pot.

"Um, the professor and I are kind of in the middle of an experiment," Frankie said. "A cooking experiment. Giant-squid stew. It's going to be deliciou-uuu-u-uuuu-u-usssss." The tentacle was shaking Frankie violently.

Just a sec!

Beatrice put the box down on the floor. "Frankie, get down from there," Beatrice commanded. "I need you to take out some garbage."

"Franki-eee!" shouted Professor Von Skalpel. "I need zee salt!" The professor had a strange accent. He always told people that he was from New Jersey, but nobody really believed him.

"Coming, Professor!" Frankie shouted. "It's kind of a bad time," Frankie said, turning to Beatrice. "Could you come back later?"

"Later—you mean after you destroy my basement?" Beatrice asked.

"Yeah," Frankie said brightly. "That would be good." Then he slammed the door in Beatrice's face.

"These monsters are driving me crazy!" Beatrice said under her breath. Then she turned and climbed the stairs to where Wolf Man Stu was jumping on Horror.

"Stop that!" Beatrice shouted. "Can't you see you're getting slime everywhere?"

But the monsters just ignored her, and Beatrice had no choice but to go around them. She'd clean the mess up later. It looked as though she wouldn't be having a moment of peace and quiet that day. The sad part is, Beatrice thought as she trudged up the stairs to her room, this is just another normal day at the Manor.

CHAPTER THREE
Haunted Toothpaste

"What's all this?" Frankie said as he held up an ancient-looking jar of eye of newt. Frankie had waited until the giant-squid stew was done. Then he had taken Beatrice's box up to his room. Next, he had pulled a pair of old underwear out of the box. "This box is full of fabulous presents!" Frankie cried.

He started taking the other things out of the box. Soon, the floor of his room was spread with old records, the skull of Beatrice's late aunt Edna, and lots of other cool stuff. Frankie grinned as he pulled the bars of stinkweed soap out of the box. "Mmm," he said, sniffing. "These smell just like Beatrice!"

Finally, there was only one thing left in the box—a crusty old green tube of something. Frankie peered at the label. "Toothpaste," he read aloud. "What's that?"

He unscrewed the top and gave the tube a big squeeze.

"Stop that!" cried a voice.

Frankie stared at the tube. Had it just said something to him? Frankie wasn't sure, so he gave the tube another squeeze.

"Aaaaaah!" the voice shouted as a blob of green, minty goo oozed from the tube. In a flash, the ooze had formed into a strange little creature in a formal suit.

Frankie jumped back in fear. "What *are*

you?" he cried, staring at the green beast.

"I'm the butler," the creature replied. "Fred."

"The . . . the butler?" Frankie repeated. He had never seen a butler before. For some reason, Frankie hadn't suspected that a butler would have small bats' wings or a tail. He also hadn't realized that a butler would smell so minty-fresh.

"Indeed." Fred gave a low bow. "My master, Allsaint Mon Staire, mistakenly stuffed

me into that tube of toothpaste," he explained. "Do you know where he is?"

"Allsaint . . ." Frankie said, thinking. Allsaint was the name of Beatrice Mon Staire's father. He had left the Manor years ago. "I don't know where he is," Frankie told the butler. "But Beatrice lives in the tower."

"I thank you," Fred said, bowing again.

Frankie bowed back, but the creature had already left the room. Frankie peered at the tube of toothpaste again. It certainly was some magical stuff!

"These monsters are getting out of control." Beatrice groaned as she lay sprawled across her spiderweb bedspread. "They're noisy *and* they're messy. If only there was some way to get rid of them! Then I could live in a nice, clean, quiet house. But let's face it; I'd have to do some pretty good magic to get them out of here. . . ." Beatrice walked over to her desk and picked up a thick book of spells. Quickly, she flipped through the chapter on making people disappear. "Ugh!" Beatrice said as she scanned the directions. "All of these spells are impossible! Isn't there anything that takes five minutes or less?"

Bang! Bang! Bang!

The knock made Beatrice sit bolt upright. Quickly, she sat on the book to hide it.

"Who dares to disturb me?" Beatrice cried in a deep voice. She couldn't let the monsters know that she was trying to find ways to get rid of them.

"Lady Beatrice, it's me—Fred."

"Fred?" Beatrice repeated. Suddenly a dozen happy memories floated through her mind. Fred had been the butler when her father still lived at the Manor. Beatrice had been a young girl then. She had loved to listen to Fred as he taught her about the poisonous plants that grew in the cemetery, or showed her how to make a superflaky cockroach pie.

Beatrice rushed to the door and flung it open. "Fred!" Beatrice cried as she bent down to hug the butler. "I thought you'd left with Father!"

"Well . . ." Fred admitted shyly, "he did pack me into a tube of toothpaste. But I suppose he forgot."

"He forgot his toothbrush, too," Beatrice said, wrinkling her nose. "Too bad he couldn't have packed you in a tub of stinkweed. That mint smells just awful."

Fred rolled his eyes. "Tell me about it." He cleared his throat slightly, then went on. "Still," he said, giving a low bow, "I'm proud to be back in your service."

"It's good to have you back," Beatrice said.

"Is there anything you would like me to do around the house?" Fred asked. "Perhaps wash down that puddle of glop and dog hair in the hallway?"

"Yes," Beatrice said slowly. "That would be lovely." Her mind was spinning. True, her spells weren't working. But now that Fred was back, maybe he could help her get the monsters out of the house. Then she could have the peace and quiet that she deserved—finally.

CHAPTER FOUR
The Sneaky, Sneaky Plan

"That should do it," Fred said as he walked back into Beatrice's room. He had just finished cleaning up the mess in the hall.

"Fred, have you noticed that there is a bunch of filthy, smelly, obnoxious monsters living in this manor?" Beatrice asked.

"Well," Fred said uncomfortably, "I don't know if I'd call them *smelly*. . . ."

"I have a perfect plan to get them all out of my house," Beatrice said quickly, "and you're going to help me do it."

"But why do you want them to leave?" Fred asked.

Just then, Kneecap Femur ran past the room, chased by her older brother, Bonehead. Bonehead was carrying a jar filled with a deformed green brain.

"Get it away from me!" Kneecap wailed.

"It'th got a mind of it'th own!" Bonehead cried as he held out the jar toward his sister. He had a terrible lisp.

"Come back here, you hooligans!" Professor Von Skalpel cried as he ran after the small skeletons. "Bring me back my brain!"

The house shook as the three chased one another down the stairs. Suddenly, there was a loud thud and the sound of breaking glass.

"Oopth," Bonehead said.

"My beautiful brain!" the professor wailed

loudly. "It is all over zee floor!"

Beatrice looked at Fred pointedly.

"Oh, I see," Fred said. "Well, why don't you just ask them to leave?"

"I don't want to seem rude, Fred," Beatrice lied. Of course, the *real* reason she couldn't ask the monsters to leave was that she didn't dare. Some of the monsters—like Wolf Man Stu, for example—had sharp fangs and short tempers.

"Well, you *do* come from a long line of famous witches," Fred pointed out. "Maybe you could use a spell to get rid of them."

"Er—no," Beatrice said quickly, remembering the time she had tried to turn Wolf Man Stu into a toad. She had only managed to make him slightly green. He'd gotten so furious that Beatrice had hidden in the boiler room for three days until he calmed down.

Mother is right—I *should* have paid better attention in charm school, Beatrice thought. Now I can't even make a pile of garbage disappear! "I hate to use my magic unless it's absolutely necessary, Fred," Beatrice went on. "Besides, I have a foolproof plan. But I'll need your help. . . ."

Half an hour later, a small creature roughly the size of a football trotted out of Beatrice's room.

It was Fred, of course, but Beatrice had managed to use her magic to make him slightly smaller—"spy-size," she called it. The truth was, she'd been trying to turn him into a fly, so that he could buzz around the Manor and take notes on all of the tenants. But that hadn't quite worked out.

Fred spent the next few days hiding behind drapes and beneath sofa cushions so that he could listen to the other monsters' conversations. Beatrice had told him that even the most insignificant information might be useful, so Fred paid attention to everything. And he was as invisible as the wind. None of the tenants noticed that he was there—even though they did notice that the Manor smelled rather minty all of a sudden.

Fred wrote down everything he heard and collected

things from the monsters' rooms. At the end of the week, he read his notes to Beatrice and showed her what he had found.

"Let's see," Beatrice said as she sat at her worktable, rubbing her chin thoughtfully. "In Von Skalpel's lab, you found a book on creatures of the night and a letter from Rick Slick, a record producer. Those things have potential. But let's start with the cemetery."

There were a few creatures living in the cemetery next to the Manor, including two grouchy teenage zombies named Eye-Gore and Steve. But after that day's spilled-brain incident, Beatrice was more concerned with getting rid of the Femur family. The four little skeletons lived in the tombs nearby. Bonehead and Kneecap were always causing trouble at the Manor, and their dog, Funnybone, never stopped yapping.

"The Femurs should be easy to get rid of," Beatrice told Fred, as she searched through the pile of papers he had brought her. She pulled a postcard out of the stack and held it up. On the front was a picture of the Egyptian pyramids. "'Wish you were here. Love, Uncle Maurice,'" Beatrice read at the bottom of the card. "This gives me a few ideas. Fred, go to the attic and bring me the largest Egyptian coffin you can find."

Fred nodded and hurried out of the room, while Beatrice reached for her magical pen. It had been a gift from her father, and it was one of the few magical things she owned that actually worked. Beatrice traced *Love, Uncle Maurice* with the pen, which could copy any person's handwriting.

Then she smiled softly to herself. This was a plan that would not fail.

CHAPTER FIVE
Bye-bye, Bonehead

"It'th freething in here," Bonehead Femur lisped on Monday morning. His breath came out in frosty puffs. The inside of the Femur tomb was as cold as death.

"Yeah, I'm chilled to the bone!" his sister, Kneecap, agreed as she sat up in her coffin, shivering.

"Wait till I get this fire started," Fibula Femur said as he struck a match to light the wood stove. "Then we'll be nice and toasty."

"You've been trying to light it for an hour!" Bonehead griped.

Just then, there was a knock at the door. "Mister Femur!" Beatrice cried. "Open up. I have something for you."

Fibula swung open the door and saw Beatrice struggling to hold a package that was bigger than she was.

"The postman left this at the Manor," Beatrice explained. "It's for you."

"What is it?" Kneecap cried as she leaped up from her coffin.

"Let me thee!" Bonehead shouted.

"I hope it's the new trampoline I ordered," Tibia Femur said. "I've been feeling jumpy lately."

Beatrice rolled her eyes. She wished these skeletons would stop yakking and start unwrapping! "You're taking too long!" she

cried as she grabbed the package and tore off the brown paper to reveal an ancient Egyptian coffin. The Femurs stared at it for a moment. Strangely, the coffin smelled like a mixture of mothballs and mint.

"Why would anyone send us something like this?" Fibula asked.

"Maybe you should open the lid," Beatrice suggested impatiently.

"Look!" Bonehead cried. "There'th a card!"

Fibula tore open the envelope and read aloud:

Hello, family!

I'm writing to you from the balcony of my pyramid. It's almost a hundred degrees outside, and I've taken off my wrappings so I can work on my tan! I'm sure you're freezing in those unheated tombs of yours—why don't you come for a visit? We can "hang in the crypt!"

Love,

Uncle Maurice

"Uncle Maurice wants us to come to Egypt?" Tibia asked.

"Yay, we're going to Egypt!" Bonehead cried.

"We'll see the Sphinx!" Kneecap shouted.

"And the Pyramidth!" Bonehead cheered.

"And the Thtatue of Liberty!"

"Now don't get carried away," Tibia said gently. "After all, Egypt is very far away. And I'm sure it's very expensive to get there."

"Your mother's right," Fibula said as he put the card back in its envelope. "I'm afraid Egypt is out of the question."

"But—but—did you look in the bottom of the envelope?" Beatrice asked quickly.

Fibula stared at her.

"I mean—uh—maybe it isn't as expensive as you think," Beatrice said awkwardly. "Maybe Maurice sent you some information . . . or . . . uh . . . something."

Fibula shrugged and peered into the envelope. "There *is* something in here," he said as he pulled four pieces of paper out of the bottom of the envelope.

"Train tickets to Egypt!" Tibia said as she

pulled the papers from her husband's hand. "And we're flying first-class!"

"Yay!" the children cheered.

"I didn't know you could get to Egypt on the train," Fibula said as he stared at the tickets. They didn't look like any train tickets he had ever seen before. In fact, they just looked like four slips of paper that someone had scribbled on. "What do you think of these, Beatrice? Do they look authentic?"

"Oh, that's how they make tickets in Egypt," Beatrice said smoothly. "They're very old-fashioned there."

"Well, okay," Fibula said with a shrug. "Then I guess we're off to Egypt!"

Beatrice smiled from ear to ear as the children cheered. It's nice to make people happy, Beatrice thought. Especially when those people are *me*.

"Did it work, my lady?" Fred asked when Beatrice returned to her room.

"Like a charm," Beatrice said. "I convinced them to grab their dog and pile into the coffin so that Frankie could carry them to the train station."

"Genius!" Fred cried. "Their uncle has no idea that they are coming! No one will release them from the coffin—they'll be stuck on a train platform in Egypt until the end of time!"

Beatrice smiled smugly and walked over to her desk. She pulled a piece of paper out of the top drawer. "Fred," she said, "it's time to move on to part two of my plan. I'm going to pay a visit to the radioactive swamp. Meanwhile, you should run over to Ivan Tagetcha, the undertaker. Tell him that you're a fabulously rich potential client, and ask him for a few brochures. . . ."

Beatrice made up her mind that she was finally going to get some peace and quiet.

CHAPTER SIX
Later, Skaters

Peace and quiet, however, were not going to be achieved quickly.

"Where have you been?" Fred asked as Beatrice staggered into her room. Her hair was messy, and she looked tired.

"Ugh, I just spent the afternoon listening to Horror play all the greatest dance hits of the nineteen-eighties on his trumpet," Beatrice said with a groan. "I thought I was going to go crazy—or deaf—but I managed to smile through the whole thing and tell him it was great. I even helped him write this letter." She handed Fred a small envelope. "Would you mind taking it to the post office for me? I've got to lie down. I have a splitting headache."

Fred took the envelope. "Rick Slick, Record Producer, Nerdburg," he read aloud. "Who's that? A friend of Horror's?"

"Not exactly," Beatrice said, "although he does hang out with some *other* slimy people. Did you get those brochures from the undertaker?"

"I certainly did," Fred said, handing the brochures to Beatrice with a flourish.

"Excellent," Beatrice said, flipping through the glossy photos. She plucked a letter from her desk. "Please go put this letter on the Femurs' doorstep," she said to Fred. "But wait until you see one of those wannabe skater zombies passing by."

Fred nodded, then turned into a bat. He carried Horror's letter to the post office, then flew back to the Femurs' vault. Naturally, it was empty, because the family was on its vacation to Egypt—er, that is, to the Transylvaniaville Dump. Fred perched atop the crypt and waited.

After a few minutes, Eye-Gore passed by, carrying a boom box. He had been playing the latest album by Disturbed Spleen at top volume for the past three hours, and neither Fibula nor Tibia had come by to tell him to turn it down. Eye-Gore was suspicious. What happened to the skeletons? he wondered. Don't they care anymore?

Eye-Gore's index finger fell off as he knocked on the door to the crypt. When he bent over to pick up his finger, a small envelope fluttered down and landed by his feet.

"What's this?" Eye-Gore asked, tearing open the letter. His eyes flew across the page. Then Eye-Gore's eyeballs bounced at the end of their stalks. "Steve!" he shouted suddenly. "Get over here!"

Five minutes later, Eye-Gore and Steve were pounding on the door to Beatrice's bedroom.

"Open up!" Steve shouted. "We know you're in there!"

Beatrice pulled open the door and smiled sweetly at the zombies. "Oh, hello," she said innocently.

"What's this supposed to mean?" Eye-Gore demanded, holding up the letter he had stolen from the Femurs' crypt. It read:

Dear Fibula,

I regret to inform you that the back road leading to the cemetery will soon be made into an eight-lane highway. Your tomb will have to be torn down.

I am sorry about this, and want to assure you that I have been searching for a new home for you and your family.

I have rented a place for you at the Rest of Your Life cemetery, on Dead Street.

A brochure is enclosed.

Yours truly,

Beatrice Mon Staire

Eye-Gore flipped through the colorful brochure, which laid out the details of the Rest of Your Life cemetery. There were sound-proof tombs with excellent views of death, relaxing graves with hot-water jets, heated coffins, a golf course . . . everything the living dead could ever want!

"What about us?" Steve demanded. "We want to be relocated because of a highway!"

Steve punched Beatrice's dresser so hard that his arm fell to the floor.

"Well," Beatrice hedged, "you don't pay me any rent, so you aren't exactly my tenants. . . ."

"I'm sick of these lame excuses!" Eye-Gore shouted, pointing a finger in Beatrice's face. It was the same finger that had fallen off earlier that day, so he had to hold it in his fist to point it at her. "If those old bones have the right to live in luxury, then so do we!"

"All right, all right," Beatrice said soothingly. "You two drive a hard bargain, but I'll see what I can do. . . ."

Half an hour later, the zombies had packed their bags and were on their way to the Rest of Your Life cemetery. As they walked, Eye-Gore carefully studied a map that Beatrice had sketched for them.

"Wow, this doesn't look that close," Eye-

Gore said, as his eyeball, perched at the end of a stalk, dangled in front of the map. "We have to pass through Nerdburg and through the Haunted Hills—"

"Hmmm," Steve said. "Maybe we should have brought a snack."

From her bedroom window at the top of the Manor's tallest tower, Beatrice watched the zombies shuffle away. Fred, back in his normal form, stood beside her.

"I hope they have a lovely time," Fred said. "That cemetery looks amazing!"

Beatrice sighed. "The Manor seems quieter already." Then she turned to Fred. "The map I drew is for a place so far away that they'll be searching for a long time. The Manor will be even more charmingly quiet in no time!" Beatrice smiled to herself. Really, she thought, who needs spells when you've got a fabulous, clever brain like mine?

CHAPTER SEVEN
Sayonara, Snobula

For the next week, Beatrice didn't ask Fred to do anything—except walk around the Manor every evening in big, heavy boots. It wasn't hard, but it was sort of strange.

"Lady Beatrice," Fred asked finally, "would you please tell me why I am strolling around in circles every night?"

"You will understand everything soon enough," Beatrice assured him. "But tonight, I want you to do something extra—nail these cloves of garlic to the Manor doors."

"Garlic? Ugh!" Fred said. Like most creatures of the night, he didn't like garlic at all. Still, he couldn't refuse to do what Beatrice asked, so he grabbed the garlic and then headed outside.

Since the Femurs, Eye-Gore, and Steve were all gone, Beatrice was able to get a good seat on the living room sofa, in front of the television. Count Snobula, Professor Von Skalpel, Wolf Man Stu, and Horror were

already there, watching Must Scream TV. And of course, Snobula had to watch his favorite show later. That put Beatrice in a bad mood, but soon she would have the couch and the remote control to herself.

"Where is everybody?" Count Snobula asked, looking around. "The Femurs never miss Thursday night television."

"Zey are probably trying to escape from Horror and his trumpet noises." The professor turned to the giant ball of slime. "You sound like a jellyfish playing zee bagpipes!"

"I may sound like a jellyfish," Horror snapped back, "but soon I'll be as rich as a . . ." He thought for a minute. "As a rich jellyfish. Thanks to Beatrice, I have big plans. Just this morning, I got a letter from—"

"Has anyone else noticed strange things happening around here lately?" Beatrice asked suddenly, cutting Horror off.

"What's stranger than hanging around with a vampire, a wannabe witch, and a giant ball of slime?" Wolf Man Stu demanded.

"A few things have disappeared from my room," Beatrice said with a shrug. "That's all."

"Hmmm . . . Zat is odd," Von Skalpel said. "Now zat you mention it, a book of mine has disappeared, too. It is all about zee creatures of zee night. And I have seen some mysterious footprints in zee snow outside zee Manor."

At that moment, Frankie stumbled into the room. "I just saw a stranger nailing garlic to the front door!" Frankie shouted. "He got away before I could catch him."

"Did you recognize him?" Stu asked.

Frankie shook his head. "I just saw him from behind," he said, "but the guy had big feet and he smelled like mint."

Count Snobula's eyes grew round, and his face became even paler green than usual, but he didn't say anything.

"I'm sure it's nothing," Beatrice said quickly. "Just a superstitious villager who believes all of the rumors about this manor." She got up, stretched, and walked out of the room.

Count Snobula followed her into the hall. "Beatrice," he whispered, "may I ask—what was taken from your room?"

"Hmmm . . ." Beatrice said, scratching her head as though she were thinking. "A garlic bouquet, a wooden spear, and a lovely, ivory-handled mirror."

The count gasped. "Vampire-hunting things!" he cried. "A hater of the undead has come to the Manor. He's already taken care of the Femurs and the zombies, and I'm next on his list! I'm in danger. I can't stay here!"

"Well, my family has a little country tomb near Nerdburg," Beatrice said helpfully. "You could stay there for a while."

"Oh, thank you!" the count cried. "I'll prepare my travel coffin. But wait," he said, stopping. "How will I get there? I can't travel during the day. And even if I left tonight, I'd never make it before dawn. . . ."

"I'll take care of everything," Beatrice assured him.

Count Snobula thanked her again and hurried off.

The next morning, Beatrice handed Frankie a big package and an overnight bag. The package was large—about the size of a coffin—and heavy, almost as heavy as a person. A person wearing a cape.

"Are you sure the professor said that I should take a vacation?" Frankie asked.

"Of course he did," Beatrice lied. "You've earned it! Besides, you'll be doing me a big favor. My cousin really needs this package."

"But—" Frankie protested.

"No buts," Beatrice said. "Just walk to the bus stop and get on the 8:19 bus. Don't talk to anyone, and try not to move. Then, get off at the last stop and wait for my cousin, Rudolph.

Give him the package and come back on the next bus. Okay?"

Frankie sighed. "But won't people be frightened of me?" he asked.

"Of course not!" Beatrice said quickly. "I'll use one of my fantastic spells on you!"

With the help of a simple magic spell, a thick, woolen hood, and eight gallons of cover-up makeup, Beatrice made Frankie appear almost human. Then she assured him that he looked like a movie star and hustled him out the door.

"Heh-heh." Beatrice chuckled softly as she waved good-bye to Frankie, who had Count Snobula's vacation coffin tucked under his arm. "Cousin Rudolph—he died in 1823! He's off haunting some old castle in Poland. Frankie will never find him! That should be the end of our vampire *and* our creature."

CHAPTER EIGHT
See Ya, Swampie!

Beatrice covered her ears as she slogged across the marshy ground that led to the radioactive swamp. A sound like a car horn drowning in tapioca pudding filled the air—Horror had been blasting away on his trumpet for the better part of the day.

Peace and quiet, peace and quiet, Beatrice chanted to herself as she walked. Soon I'll have my peace and quiet.

"There you are!" Horror said as Beatrice

walked up to him. "I've been practicing!"

"So I heard," Beatrice said, placing her hand over the trumpet to stop Horror from starting up again. "You sound terrific!"

"I'm so glad you think so!" Horror glanced around the swamp. "Even the little swamp critters stopped in their tracks when they heard me."

"Mmm," Beatrice said, remembering the many limp toads she'd passed on her way out to the swamp. "You were knocking 'em dead." Beatrice cleared her throat. "And I'm sure you'll do the same thing at your audition today. Rick Slick will freak out when he hears you—I guarantee it!"

"Thanks!" Horror said happily. "And

With the money from my record sales, I can have a Jacuzzi filled with radioactive waste!

How relaxing...

thanks again for helping me write to Mr. Slick. I never could have written such a fancy letter without you."

Beatrice smiled to herself, remembering the letter that she'd written for Horror:

Dear Mr. Slick:

I am a young trumpeter with a unique style. I am comfortable with the great classics (Beethoven, Bach, the Backstreet Boys), and even perform some of my own pieces (my song "Love Gargle" is a guaranteed hit). I can also drive away cockroaches, burglars, angry dogs, and many other things within a two-mile radius. I hope you'll have time to hear me audition in the near future.

Yours truly,

H. of the Swamps

P.S.: I am a friend of Frankie's.

Beatrice didn't really understand how the professor and Frankie knew Rick Slick, but—on the other hand—she really didn't care, either. All she cared about was the fact that Rick Slick was a powerful man . . . and that Horror thought that Mr. Slick could help him with his trumpet career. Oh, I am a clever witch, Beatrice thought as she reread the letter. And even if my spells are lousy, at least my *spelling* is okay.

"Have you heard back from Mr. Slick yet?" Beatrice asked.

"Yes!" Horror held out an envelope. "It just came in the mail yesterday—Mr. Slick wants me to audition right away!"

Beatrice scanned the letter in the envelope Horror had handed her. Perfect—Rick Slick had fallen for her letter, hook, line, and sinker. He wanted to meet with Horror immediately!

Beatrice suppressed a shudder. The poor man doesn't know what he's getting into, she thought.

"This is wonderful, Horror," Beatrice said, pulling a large, plastic rain poncho out of her bag. "Here," she said, handing it to Horror. "Put this on and pull up the hood, so that you can go to Nerdburg without frightening anyone. You know how mean people can be to monsters! But I'm sure Mr. Slick will judge you solely on your talent."

"Thanks, Beatrice!" Horror said, slipping the rain poncho over his head. "How can I ever thank you? Oh! I know—I'll play you an

original song, 'Swamp Stomp Boogie!'"

"No!" Beatrice cried, then stopped herself. "That is—you don't have time!"

"Good point!" Horror said. "What if Mr. Slick finds another talented trumpet player before I even get a chance to audition?"

"You just can't let that happen!" Beatrice urged. "You'd better get to the road right away, so the bus can pick you up!"

Beatrice watched as Horror hurried off toward the road. He looked like a garbage bag full of jelly as he wiggled and jiggled inside his plastic poncho.

Inside the Manor, Beatrice listened to the joyful silence. She was very close to her goal of peace and quiet.

CHAPTER NINE
Au Revoir, Professor

"Fred, we're almost finished," Beatrice said as she handed him an envelope.

"Is this my paycheck?" Fred asked hopefully.

"Um, no," Beatrice said. "That is a letter for Professor Von Skalpel, which you are going to leave on Frankie's bed. Then, you'll go down to the laboratory and make a mess." Beatrice handed Fred a screwdriver.

"It sounds like I'm going to have a busy afternoon," Fred said.

Beatrice grinned. This was one mess she was actually looking forward to. "You'd better get started."

Professor Von Skalpel was busy in his lab, trying to get a rat to taste his latest chewing-gum flavor—onion–peppermint–maple walnut. The rat wasn't interested.

"Perhaps I should experiment with new meat flavors," the professor mused.

Crash!

The professor jumped as a heavy shelf of toxic chemicals and household cleaning products fell behind him. "Vhat is going on?" he cried as the chemicals mixed together, hissing and gurgling on the tile floor. That was when the professor noticed that some of the chemicals looked about to react—and explode! "Uh-oh. Zees is not good." The professor grabbed his rat and ran.

"Frankie!" Professor Von Skalpel screamed as he bolted from the lab. "Clean up in aisle one!"

There was no reply.

"Frankie?" the professor repeated. The Manor was strangely silent. After a moment, Professor Von Skalpel heard a shuffling noise behind him. "Frankie!" he said, turning around.

"Guess again," said a gruff voice. It was Wolf Man Stu.

"Oh, it is you, Schtu," the professor said. "Have you seen Frankie?" The floor shook as something exploded in the lab. "Uh, I have some vork for him to do," the professor explained, "but I cannot find him anyvhere."

"You mean he's disappeared, too?" Stu asked. "That means we're the only two left—except for Beatrice."

"Vhat are you talking about?" Professor Von Skalpel asked. Feeling suddenly nervous, the professor began to climb the stairs to Frankie's room. "Frankie?" he called.

"Haven't you noticed that everyone else has disappeared?" Stu growled. "And that the house still smells like mint?"

But the professor wasn't listening. Noticing a letter on Frankie's bed, he picked it up. It was the same letter that Rick Slick had sent to the Swamp Horror, which Beatrice had swiped from him earlier that morning. But the professor didn't know that. That was why he felt ill as he read:

I received your letter and would love to meet with you. Come to Nerdburg right away and we'll do lunch.

Yours truly,
Rick Slick

"Zis is horrible!" Professor Von Skalpel groaned. "Frankie has gone to Nerdburg!" Frankie had a wonderful singing voice and killer dance moves—and Von Skalpel was his agent. If Frankie met with Rick Slick directly, Von Skalpel wouldn't get his share of the money Frankie made from recording CDs.

"Give me that," Stu said, ripping the paper from the scientist's hands. Stu gave the paper a sniff. "Mint!" he cried. "I knew it! This is a fake! Beatrice is behind this, I'm telling you!"

"No, it is real," the professor insisted. "I know Rick Slick's letters. Zis is his paper, and zis is his signature, I am sure of it. I have got to stop Frankie from meeting viz him!" The professor hurried out of the room.

The werewolf followed him. "Don't go!" Stu cried. "It's a trap!"

"I cannot risk it," the professor said. "If Rick Slick meets Frankie, he vill have a new recording contract, and I vill not have a cent. Or an assistant!"

Stu growled, but there was nothing he could do. The professor had already scurried out the front door.

"There he goes," Beatrice said as she looked out her bedroom window. Even though darkness was falling, she could still see the professor as he ran across the front lawn.

"Good luck finding Frankie in Nerdburg, little professor," she added cheerfully. "You'll be looking for a long time!"

"My lady is a genius," Fred said with a low bow. "I suppose you already have a plan for kicking out the werewolf?"

"Of course, Fred," Beatrice replied, as she pulled a book from the top drawer of her desk. It was *Creatures of the Night*, the book that Fred had swiped from the professor's lab a few weeks ago. "Werewolves are very dangerous, as you know," Beatrice said, flipping through the pages. "But all we have to do is wait for—"

Thud! Thud! Thud!

Beatrice stopped to listen. Heavy footsteps were coming up the staircase. There was no doubt about it—the werewolf was on his way.

CHAPTER TEN
Adieu, Stu

"Don't let him in, Fred!" Beatrice called. "It's too soon!"

"Never fear, my lady!" Fred cried. "I'll pound him to a pulp. He'll never get past m—"

The door flew open, smashing Fred against the wall.

"I knew it!" Wolf Man Stu shouted as he burst into the room. "It smells minty in here! Beatrice, you've got some explaining to do!"

"Of course," Beatrice said slowly as she rose

from her desk. Ever so casually, she slipped the book off her desk and backed toward the window. "I can explain everything," she went on, "for, you see—eeek!" And with that, Beatrice jumped out the window.

Wolf Man Stu jumped after her.

"AAAAAHHH!" Beatrice and Wolf Man Stu cried as they fell toward the ground.

Thud! Thud!

They landed at the edge of the radioactive swamp. The werewolf instantly leaped to his feet and growled.

Beatrice held out the book of spells. "Stay back!" she shouted. "I have a book, and I'm not afraid to use it!"

Stu let out a noise that was half snarl, half laugh. "You think I'm afraid of your book of spells?"

69

he demanded. "Your magic is as weak as an earthworm in a body cast!"

With lightning speed, Beatrice lifted the book and—whacked Stu over the head with it.

"I didn't see that coming," Wolf Man Stu said as he fell to the ground. Normally, he would have barely felt a little book-whacking. But just moments earlier, under the light of the full moon, he had turned from a horrifying werewolf into a pudgy little man. That's right—Wolf Man Stu was just . . . well . . . plain old Stu.

"Lady Beatrice!" Fred called as he came running from the Manor. "Are you all right?"

"I'm fine," Beatrice replied, "thanks to you."

"But I didn't do anything," Fred said.

"Yes, you did. You brought me this book," Beatrice said, pointing to a page she held open.

"I did?" Fred asked. "When?"

"Way back in chapter four," Beatrice replied. "But that's not important right now. It says right here that there is a very rare kind of werewolf that can turn into a human when the moon is full. I realized that Stu here," she said, pointing to the little man who lay on the frozen snow, "is one of those werewolves. I knew that I just had to wait for the right moment to strike!"

"Brilliant!" Fred cried.

"Yes," Beatrice agreed, with a smug little smile. "Yes, I suppose I am." She grinned as she watched the butler haul away the used-to-be wolf man. I guess I do know a little magic, Beatrice thought. After all, I do know how to make things disappear!

CHAPTER ELEVEN
And Then There Was . . . One?

"**E**xcuse me, my lady," Fred said, "but it seems that I have a score to settle with the—er—used–to–be wolf man." He frowned, remembering how Stu had squished him behind the door.

"Okay!" Beatrice said. "But don't do anything fancy. Just tie him up and take him someplace far away."

"Absolutely," Fred agreed. "I'll take him to a deserted island!" He grunted as he struggled to haul the former werewolf into a wheelbarrow. "Er—well—maybe I'll just take him to the dump," Fred said, once the wheelbarrow was loaded. "He is pretty heavy."

Beatrice walked toward the Manor as the wheelbarrow squeaked away behind her. At last, she had the Manor all to herself. Beatrice could finally have some peace and quiet. She could tend to her beautiful, poisonous plants instead of cleaning up after a bunch of sloppy monsters. And she could watch whatever she wanted on TV.

But as Beatrice walked into the Manor, a sound stopped her in her tracks. *What's this?* Beatrice wondered. *I thought my house was going to be peaceful and quiet!* But someone was already sitting on the couch in front of the television, watching *Ghoul House* and singing the idiotic theme song at the top of her lungs.

Good-bye.

You're not bad . . .

but Snow White had a much cuter hairstyle!

It was Beatrice's mother, Sally! She's been invisible for weeks, Beatrice thought, clenching her teeth. She had to pick *this* moment to show up?

"Hey, Bea!" Sally chirped. "Where is everybody?"

"Everyone's gone," Beatrice snapped.

"What?" Sally cried. "I thought they'd all be watching the show!" She turned back to the TV and laughed when one of the actors slipped on a banana peel and then got doused by a bucket of slime. "Ooh, that's funny."

"Oh, forget it, Mother," Beatrice said, storming up the stairs. "I have to go practice a few spells. I'll see you later."

Beatrice stormed up to her bedroom and locked the door. Then she flopped onto her bed. Even though she could still hear the television blaring downstairs, the house was unusually quiet. And tidy. And for the first time in years, there were no monsters to yell at or messes to clean up. Beatrice realized with a start that she really didn't have anything to do.

I guess I'd better find a way to get rid of Mother, Beatrice decided. After all, she was bored. Still, she hesitated a moment. If she got rid of Sally, Beatrice really would be all alone. Was that what she wanted?

"Lady Beatrice!" Fred shouted as he burst into the room, cutting off Beatrice's thoughts. "We have a slight problem!"

CHAPTER TWELVE
It All Comes Back to Haunt Her in the End

*F*red turned to close the door behind him, but he was too slow. There was a deafening noise as Frankie stomped into the room, followed by the Swamp Horror, the zombies, the Femurs, and Count Snobula. Von Skalpel was the last to storm in. He was carrying non–Wolf Man Stu on his back. Now that Stu was out of the moonlight, he quickly turned back into his usual furry self.

Beatrice couldn't help grinning at the sight of her friends. My goodness, she thought, I think I've actually missed them! Beatrice cleared her throat. "Oh, hi," she said casually. "Where've you all been?"

The creatures all started to talk at once.

"My magic beauty spell started to smear in the rain," Frankie said, "so I didn't dare take the bus."

"I found Horror and Frankie on zee road to Nerdburg," Professor Von Skalpel explained. "Zey told me zey vere going to see Rick Slick, but I explained vhy zat vas a very bad idea."

"I tried to tell the professor that I wasn't going to see Mr. Slick at all," Frankie protested. "I told him that I was delivering a package for you. But then we heard a noise from inside the package—"

"—And they finally let me out!" Count

Snobula finished Frankie's sentence.

"Steve and I found a coffin in the ditch near the dump," Eye-Gore said. "When we opened it, we found the Femurs. Boy, Tibia almost lost her head!"

"We didn't even get to thee the Thtatue of Liberty," Bonehead complained. "The only green perthon we thaw wath *that* little guy"— Bonehead pointed to Fred—"carrying Thtu to the dump in a wheelbarrow."

"I don't remember anything!" Stu said with a groan, as he rubbed his head. "Where am I?"

"Hey, that's the little guy I saw in my room!" Frankie shouted suddenly, looking at Fred. "The minty one!"

"Silence!" Beatrice commanded, holding up her hand. She looked around at the noisy bunch of monsters. "I see that you all have questions," she said to her monster tenants. "And you deserve the truth. The truth is . . ." She paused, and looked around the room. Everyone was staring at her. What am I going to tell them? Beatrice thought. I can't tell them the truth—then they might leave for good! Beatrice was surprised to realize that she didn't want her friends to leave. But how could she get them to stay? Her eyes fell on Fred, who was blinking up at her. He gave her an encouraging smile. Suddenly, Beatrice had an idea. "The truth is that Fred here has been trying to get rid of you!" she shouted.

The monsters gasped. Fred gasped the loudest.

"I'm sure that you were planning to get rid of me, too!" Beatrice added, turning to face the butler. "Thankfully, my good friends came back in time to stop you!"

"But, Lady Beatrice," Fred said weakly. "You—"

"Yes, you're right!" Beatrice shouted. "I'm the one who will punish you!" She held up the empty mustard jar. "*Alaca-zudding, alaca-zustard!* Put this butler into the mustard!"

In a flash, the little green butler disappeared. After a moment, everyone could hear a weak tapping coming from the inside of the mustard jar as Beatrice screwed the lid back on tight.

"There!" Beatrice said happily. "Fred won't be causing any more problems!"

No one knew what to say.

The professor cleared his throat. "Well . . ." he said finally, "I guess zat is zat."

"Oh, good! You're all back," Sally said as she appeared in the room. "Who wants to play a game?"

"I do!" Horror shouted.

"Me, too! Me, too!" cried the Femur kids.

It turned out that everyone was in the mood for a game. The monsters thundered down the stairs to gather inside the living room. Sally turned up the stereo while Frankie and the zombies set up the game board. Everyone was talking and laughing at once, and the Manor was noisier than it had been in weeks. Strangely, Beatrice didn't find the noise annoying. In fact, it was kind of comforting. And even though Beatrice was sure that there would be a huge mess to clean up after the monsters finished their game—and their evening snacks—she didn't really mind. At least having a house full of monsters is never boring, Beatrice thought. Maybe trying to get rid of everyone was a mistake, after all. . . .

"Beatrice!" Sally called from downstairs. "It's your turn!"

"I'll be right there!" Beatrice shouted. Then she dropped her voice. "Don't worry," she whispered to the jar of mustard as she hid it in the back of her sock drawer. "I promise to let you out . . . eventually. And look at it this way—at least you won't smell like mint anymore!"